For Dash & Becks

The Big Ideas of Buster Bickles
Copyright © 2015 by Dave Wasson
All rights reserved. Manufactured in China.
No part of this book may be used or reproduced in any manner whatsoever without
written permission except in the case of brief quotations embodied in critical articles
and reviews. For information address HarperCollins Children's Books, a division of
HarperCollins Publishers, 195 Broadway, New York, NY 10007.
www.harpercollinschildrens.com

ISBN 978-0-06-229178-3

The artist used Adobe Flash to create the digital illustrations for this book.
Typography by Jeff Shake
15 16 17 18 19 SCP 10 9 8 7 6 5 4 3 2 1
❖
First Edition

THE BIG IDEAS OF Buster Bickles

by Dave Wasson

HARPER

An Imprint of HarperCollinsPublishers

From the moment he woke up,
Buster Bickles was full of big ideas.

"Hey, Mom, look! I'm a flesh-eating robot!"

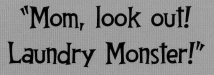

"Mom, look out! Laundry Monster!"

"Hey, Mom! **EGGS**-ray vision!"

"Buster, stop fooling around or you'll miss the bus," Mom yelled.

WAITTTTTTTTT!

poooOf!

He made it just in the nick of time for show-and-tell.

"No one seems to like my ideas, Mom," Buster said sadly.

"Why don't we visit Uncle Roswell?
He'll understand. He always has a lot of big ideas."

"Aww, Bunsen burners!" shouted Uncle Roswell.

"Is something wrong?" Buster asked.
"Not just wrong," his uncle exclaimed. "It's stupendously, horrendously, tremendously wrong! Come this way."

"**Whoa!** What is that thing?!?" asked Buster.
"I call it the **What-if Machine!**"
his uncle proclaimed.

"It makes anything you can imagine into reality!
But I need some big ideas to test it, and
I can't think of any."

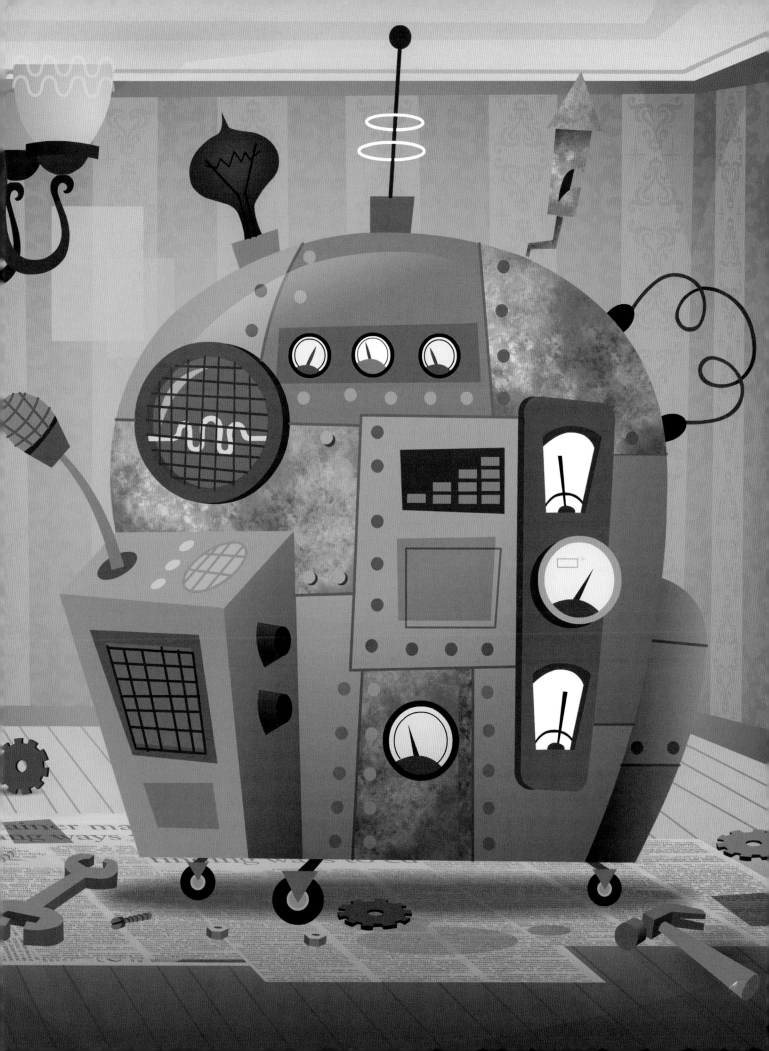

"Say, you wouldn't have any big ideas,
would you?" asked his uncle.

"Do I have any ideas? Boy, do I ever!" Buster said.

As Buster began, the machine kicked into gear.

WHAT IF...

... I had a giant mustache!

OR ... we were invisible!

OR ... we could walk on the ceiling!

OR ... it was raining guinea pigs!

OR ... I had a hat made of cheese!

OR ... we had little tiny heads!

OR ... we were wild monkeys!

OR ... we traveled by rocket-powered cow!"

Then Buster had an even **BIGGER** idea.

"What if the world was made of

ICE CREAM!"

And all at once it was!
There was even a caramel river!

And then Buster wondered, "What if our neighborhood was filled with **ROBOT DINOSAURS!**"

"Extraordinary!" exclaimed Uncle Roswell.
"I wonder if they're friendly."

They weren't.

"What-if Machine, get us as far away from here as possible!" Buster yelled.

"**YIKES!**" gulped Uncle Roswell.

$\pi = mc^2$

"I—I wish we were back home!" Buster shouted.
But the machine just sat there.

$$@^2 + \%_0^2 = \#^2$$

"The What-if Machine has drifted too far away!"
said Uncle Roswell. "It can't hear us!"

. . . and suddenly everything was back to normal.

"Brilliant! Stupendous! You saved us," Uncle Roswell said after the smoke had cleared. "If there's anything I can do for you, Buster, just ask."

"Well," said Buster, "actually, there might be. . . ."

And from that day forward nobody ever laughed at Buster's BIG ideas again.

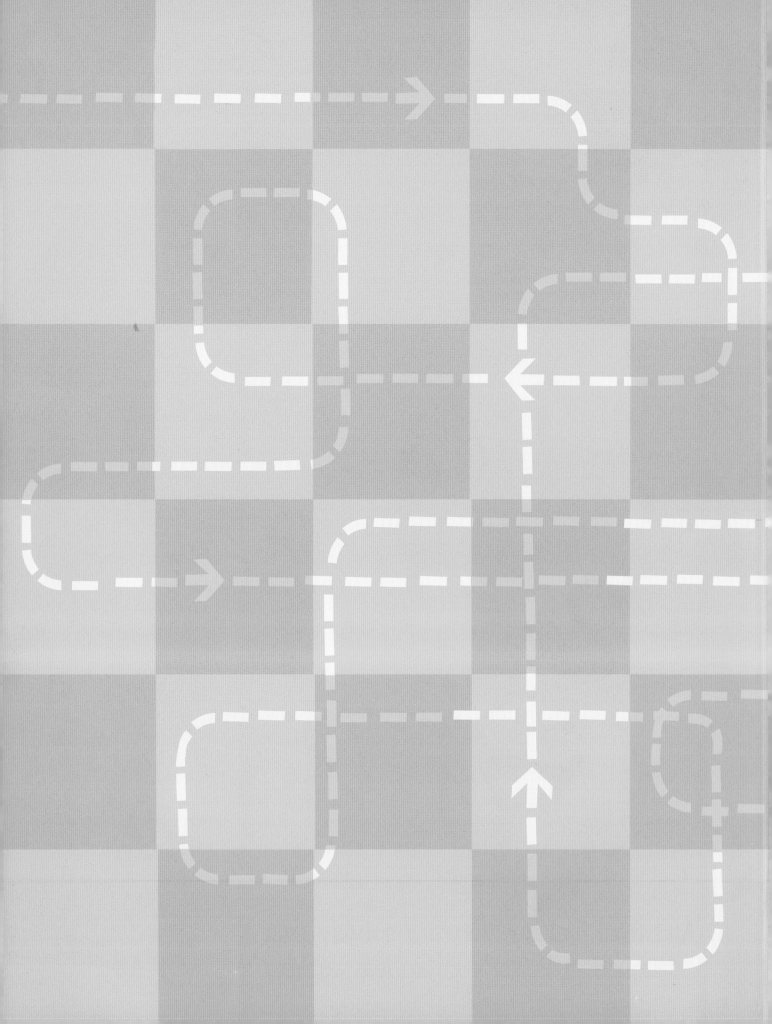